Skye
Morgan
Teri
Lana
Kiyana
Eloise
Trevon
Miles
Sophie
Elisa
Ryder
Hazel
Lee
Lincoln
Luis
Owen
Bao
Rio
Waldo
Laura
Luke
Dakota
Huong
Caitlin
Helga
Ajani
Lido
Hugo
Simon
Ivy
Marie-Elena
Serena
Deva
Tyrell
Niko
Fiona
Latonya
Devi
Lyra
Dae
Audrey
Tien
Vanessa
Jose
Delphine
Enola
Corrie
Lola
Benjamin
Mario
Malik
Jorge
Azi
Rita
Gianna
Poppy
Enzo
Zelda
Myles
Scout
Darnell
Tanisha
Shine
Lexi
Cloud
Evelyn
Misha
Khalid
Drew
Allan
Rafael
Shima
Liz
Jamila
Mei
Cleo
Arlo
Miguel
Fritz
Helena
Meilani
Ember
Royce
Rachel
Miller
Alma
Sophia
Sarah
Idris
Luella
Daisy
Nellie
Wren
Jack
Lazaro
Talia
Divya
Nava
Ezra
Sef
Paul
Carlos
Ana
Lena
Amy
Alvaro
Juana
Isaac
Wilbur
Zane
Daniel
Dylan
Antonia
Sienna

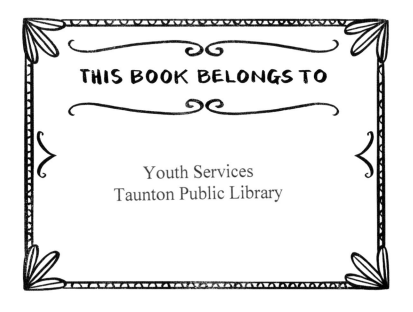

THIS BOOK BELONGS TO

Youth Services
Taunton Public Library

With gratitude to Autumn, Cameron, Cecilia, Claire, Olive, Samantha, and Shine from the Young Editors Project

First edition 2022

Library of Congress Catalog Card Number 2022930423
ISBN 978-1-5362-1856-5

22 23 24 25 26 27 APS 10 9 8 7 6 5 4 3 2 1

Printed in Humen, Dongguan, China

This book was typeset in American Typewriter.
The illustrations were created using traditional printmaking methods and assembled digitally.

Candlewick Press
99 Dover Street
Somerville, Massachusetts 02144

www.candlewick.com

3 2872 50191 9132

WHAT'S YOUR NAME?

Bethanie Deeney Murguia

CANDLEWICK PRESS

Everyone has one . . .
or maybe a few.

So what's in a name?

What does it do?

A name is a meeting,

a greeting,

a call.

A name looks for comfort
after a fall.

A name is a question,

a warning,

a taunt.

A name has the power
to worry, to haunt.

A name can be common, familiar, and known.

A name can be rare,
unique, all your own.

Names honor family
and athletes and stars—
people through history
and heroes of ours.

Names can be chosen for all kinds of reasons:
the place of your birth, the changing of seasons,

the day you were born, the planets' positions,
the time you appeared, the weather conditions.

Imagine a world
where you were called You.
And I was named You.
And they were You, too.

How would that go?
What do you think?
I'm not asking you,
rather you—in the pink.

Perhaps a name shapes the way people see you—

if it were different, would you still **be** you?

Whiskers

Fluffy

Do people and critters grow into their names—

Dash

Zen

Just breathe.

Cupid

Trouble

becoming alike, one and the same?

Midnight

Melody

Or is there a chance your name doesn't match?

What happens then? Can you detach?

You might try new names, or add on a bit,

give them a whirl, and see how they fit.

Or maybe a name for each situation:

a spy name,

a stage name,

a name for creations.

Plus names that are secret
between you and me—
nicknames invented,
a friendship decree.

Names can be whispers or music or roars.

Or proud declarations—so tell me . . .

what's yours?

Zachariah
Hudson
Jo
Reese
Yumi
Kendra
Riya
Kira
Heidi
Oliver
Catalina
Alyssa
Declan
Felipe
Jordan
Bo
Livy
Zoe
Max
Erika
Gabriela
Lashawn
Nora
Alvin
Aya
Kiara
Ira
Sage
Ivan
Flynn
Nita
Mia
Apollo
Heidi
Ozzie
Jenna
Wyatt
Tyler
Barbara
Maurice
Shin
Anton
Alejandra
Aki
Tyrone
Roy
Clara
Lucy
Olivia
Jada
Myo
Winona
Quinn
Maya
Lex
Mila
Nia
Xavier
Eli
Kendall
Rubin
Opal
Alina
Jackson
Sunny
Savannah
Ama
Fernando
Henry
Drake
Denzel
Araceli
Ella
Bora
Rivka
Luka
Tamar
Ian
Patrick
Angel
Stella
Maverick
Zack
Ophelia
Malia
Noel
Hanifa